THE SILVER SECRET

READ ALL OF THE
ENCHANTING ADVENTURES!

SNOW SISTERS

THE SILVER SECRET

By **Astrid Foss**

Illustrated by **Monique Dong**

ALADDIN

NEW YORK LONDON TORONTO SYDNEY NEW DELHI

ALADDIN

An imprint of Simon & Schuster Children's Publishing Division
1230 Avenue of the Americas, New York, New York 10020
First Aladdin paperback edition December 2020
Text copyright © 2018 by Working Partners Ltd
Cover illustrations copyright © 2020 by Sharon Tancredi
Interior illustrations copyright © 2018 by Monique Dong
Originally published in Great Britain in 2018 by Nosy Crow Ltd
Also available in an Aladdin hardcover edition.
All rights reserved, including the right of reproduction in whole or in part in any form.
ALADDIN and related logo are registered trademarks of Simon & Schuster, Inc.
For information about special discounts for bulk purchases, please contact Simon & Schuster
Special Sales at 1-866-506-1949 or business@simonandschuster.com.
The Simon & Schuster Speakers Bureau can bring authors to your live event.
For more information or to book an event contact the Simon & Schuster Speakers Bureau
at 1-866-248-3049 or visit our website at www.simonspeakers.com.
Cover designed by Heather Palisi
The text of this book was set in GaramondDTInfant
Manufactured in the United States of America 1020 OFF
2 4 6 8 10 9 7 5 3 1
Library of Congress Cataloging-in-Publication Data
Names: Foss, Astrid, author. | Dong, Monique, illustrator. | Title: The silver secret / Astrid Foss;
illustrated by, Monique Dong. | Description: New York : Aladdin Books, 2020. | Series: Snow
sisters ; 1 | Originally published in London by Nosy Crow in 2018. | Audience: Grades 4–6 |
Audience: Ages 7–10 | Summary: As they celebrate their twelfth birthday in the wintry world of
Nordovia, triplets Hanna, Magda, and Ida acquire magic powers and a mission to rescue their
parents, defeat the evil Shadow Witch, and find the pink Everchanging Light.
Identifiers: LCCN 2019042155 (print) | LCCN 2019042156 (ebook) |
ISBN 9781534443488 (paperback) | ISBN 9781534443495 (hardcover) | ISBN 9781534443501 (ebook)
Subjects: CYAC: Sisters—Fiction. | Triplets—Fiction. | Magic—Fiction. | Snow—Fiction. |
Adventure and adventurers—Fiction.
Classification: LCC PZ7.1.F672 Si 2020 (print) | LCC PZ7.1.F672 (ebook) | DDC [Fic]—dc23
LC record available at https://lccn.loc.gov/2019042155
LC ebook record available at https://lccn.loc.gov/2019042156

Prologue

Though the sun had begun to sink below the horizon, the Everchanging Lights sent fresh colour dancing across the sky above the beautiful island of Nordovia. Hanna, Magda, and Ida smiled as they waved their parents farewell from the window of their bedchamber.

Freya and Magnus Aurora were to be guests of honor at a banquet in neighboring Icefloss, as a thank-you for their help in protecting the town from that winter's harsh snowstorms.

"Your father and I will return in the morning for your birthday celebrations," Freya called to the triplets. "If you misbehave, the Lights will let me know!"

As if in response, the purple, blue, and pink lights in the sky glowed more brightly for a moment.

"We'll be good, Mother!" called Ida, jostling for a place at the window between her sisters.

"Well, we'll try! Don't watch the Lights too closely!" giggled Hanna.

"Bye, Mother! Bye, Father!" cried Magda, watching Freya and Magnus trudge away through the deep snow toward their sleigh. The two Arctic wolves that pulled it were shaking their harnesses, impatient to be off.

The girls' mother had a very special role on Nordovia. She was the Keeper of the Lights. The magical Everchanging Lights sustained and protected the island, and the Aurora family had

been in charge of their magic for as long as anyone could remember. The Keepers of the Lights kept everything in balance, guiding the magic to care for everything that lived on the island, and looking after the people. Hanna, Magda, and Ida knew that one day it would be their turn to take on this responsibility.

The girls stayed huddled together at the window, following the lantern on their parents' sleigh until it disappeared from view in the dusk.

As Freya Aurora settled back into the sleigh, she took Magnus's hand. She could hardly believe that their girls were to turn twelve the next day—the age at which they would come into their magical powers, just as she had done. She couldn't wait to see what each girl would be able to do. Each Aurora's power was different. Freya had been thrilled to discover her ability to momentarily freeze time—though it had taken her a while to learn how to use her gift. She frowned as she thought about her sister, who had come into her own power a year later and had chosen a very different path. . . .

Magnus squeezed her hand and smiled warmly, before turning to shout a loud "Yah!" to hurry the wolves along. Although he had no magic of his own, Magnus was a strong and brave man, who led his guardsmen well and helped the people of Nordovia in any way he could.

The pair talked happily as Magnus drove the wolves through the woodland, Freya's red hair streaming behind her like flickering flames in the cold air. But as they approached the heart of the forest, the two white wolves suddenly drew to a halt.

"What is it, boys?" called Magnus. "On!"

But the wolves seemed frozen, and whimpered in fright.

Magnus climbed down from the carriage, stroking his blond beard in confusion.

"Something feels wrong . . . ," Freya said in concern. "Be careful, Husband."

The wolves had come to a halt in a small clearing. To one side, a steep bank of rock jutted above the trees, and the dark entrance to a cave gaped at its base. Now the wolves began to growl at the mouth of the cave. Freya leaped from the carriage to join her husband, and as the pair crept toward the shadowy entrance, Magnus drew his sword and Freya readied her magic. Their footsteps quietened as they stepped inside the cave.

There was no longer snow beneath their feet, just dirt and dried pine needles. They stood for a moment, waiting for their eyes to adjust to the darkness.

"Who's there?" called Magnus. "Show yourself!"

The shallow cave echoed Magnus's words back at him. They searched around but the cave seemed empty, and the pair walked back through the entrance. But as Freya stepped into the dim light, a shadow emerged from the trees and grasped her wrist tightly.

But it wasn't a shadow. It was a woman.

Her hair—the colour of a starless night sky—spilled around her pale face. In her left hand she held a gleaming staff, as clear and smooth as glass.

Or ice.

"Veronika!" cried Freya. Fear flooded through her. She tried to use her magic to freeze time but her sister had cast a spell with her grip, blocking her power. As she struggled to

escape, Magnus ran to help her, but Veronika stabbed her staff into the ground and shouted a vicious-sounding spell. Instantly, gnarled tree limbs burst out of the snow and weaved themselves around him. The thick tree limbs writhed around, squeezing Magnus's hand and forcing him to drop his blade. He was trapped. Distracted by Magnus, Veronika's grip on Freya's arm loosened. Freya seized her chance and rapidly muttered a powerful spell of her own. Three orbs shot from Freya's free hand and into the dark sky. The Everchanging

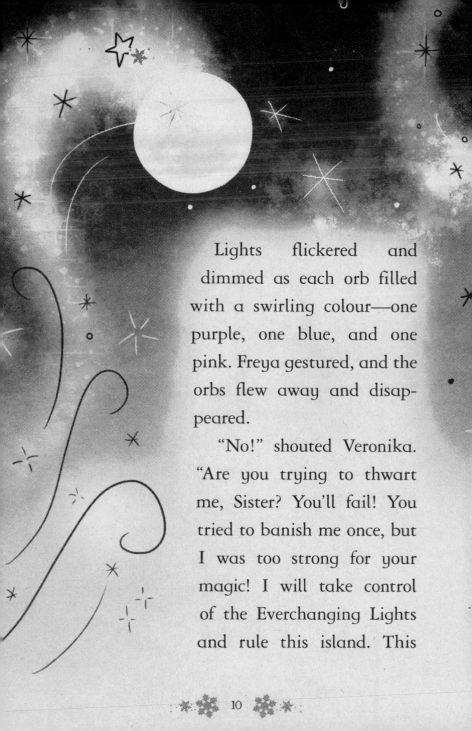

Lights flickered and dimmed as each orb filled with a swirling colour—one purple, one blue, and one pink. Freya gestured, and the orbs flew away and disappeared.

"No!" shouted Veronika. "Are you trying to thwart me, Sister? You'll fail! You tried to banish me once, but I was too strong for your magic! I will take control of the Everchanging Lights and rule this island. This

time you will not succeed in stopping me!"

She opened her lips and a stream of words flowed forth in a hoarse whisper.

Freya recognized them for what they were: a curse. Veronika was using it to drain Freya's magic from her.

The woman laughed—an eerie, throaty sound—and Freya's eyes widened with fear. Veronika, the Shadow Witch, had returned to Nordovia, and she was more powerful, more evil, than ever before.

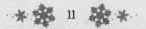

Chapter One

The triplets raced down the castle's west passage toward their bedchamber, late to the preparations for their birthday celebration. As usual, Hanna was up ahead, laughing and pulling her sisters Ida and Magda by the hands.

"Stop tugging!" shouted Magda.
"We'd have been back on time if you'd left the skating pond earlier, Hanna," Ida pointed out.

"It's our birthday!" Hanna shot back. "I deserve to have some fun!"

Ida rolled her eyes, but kept running. She had spent a peaceful morning drawing a beautiful snow orchid that had just begun to bloom among the nearby spruce trees. That is, until the wild deer Magda had been playing with had run right through the glade and crushed the little flower. But there was no time for arguing about that now. Madame Olga, their governess, would be waiting. She always told them that being the daughters of the Keeper of the Lights was no excuse for being late!

Hanna, still dragging her sisters, sped past two of the castle maids scrubbing windows, who called out birthday good wishes to the girls.

Suddenly Magda slowed down and came to a stop in front of an enormous tapestry.

"What?" asked Hanna, impatient.

"Yes, come on, I want to see our new dresses!" added Ida.

But Magda was studying the wall hanging, which she loved. She freed her hand from her sister's. "You do think Mother and Father are all right, don't you?"

The girls shared a long look, their identical green eyes locked. It was hours into their birthday morning, and their parents still hadn't returned to the castle. It wasn't like them to be gone this long without sending word, especially on the girls' special day. No one was saying it out loud, but something didn't feel right.

Ida turned to look at the tapestry. It was the Nordovian flag. The castle was filled with rare and beautiful items—a sculpture of an ancient tree carved from a single glittering chunk of volcanic rock, a huge crystal vase filled with hundreds of snowy lily-of-the-valley flowers that never wilted. But the girls all loved this tapestry best. Ida reached out to touch the intricate designs. With one finger she traced the glittering crystal rose, the majestic snow hawk, the perfect circle of a full rainbow: all ancient symbols of Nordovia. It made her feel better. She gave a small sigh. Maybe everything would be fine.

"Everything *will* be fine," Hanna said out

loud, as if she had read her sister's thoughts. "I'm sure Mother and Father will be back any minute." Her expression turned mischievous. "So . . . have either of you felt any magic yet?" she asked.

Magda shook her head. "For a moment this morning I thought I made the clouds move, but it was just the wind!"

Her sisters laughed.

"No, nothing yet," said Ida. "I hope I get something nice!"

"I hope I get something exciting!" Hanna replied with a grin.

Ida rolled her eyes, but then her gaze drifted up to the sky outside the window. "Have you noticed anything strange about the Everchanging Lights? They don't look right."

Hanna and Magda joined their sister at the window as Ida continued. "Usually they're happy and alive, but now they seem sort of faded. The pretty blue light keeps coming and going—look! It keeps fading into a kind of grayish—"

"Ida." Hanna reached out and took her sister's hand, giving it a warm squeeze. She knew Ida was getting lost in worried thoughts. Hanna forced her own fears to the back of her mind. "Of course Mother and Father are fine. Do you know anyone stronger than Father, or more clever than Mother? She's the Keeper of the Lights; can you imagine anything that could compete with her magic?"

Ida smiled a little and shook her head.

"Of course not," said Magda. "The Lights are probably just dimming because Mother knows we're late for getting ready, and she's warning us!"

Ida and Hanna laughed.

"Besides," Hanna reminded her, "Mother and Father wouldn't miss our twelfth birthday for anything! They've probably stopped to get more presents for us. A new pair of skis for me, a beautiful saddle for Magda, . . . and a big boring *easel* for you, so you can sit and draw pictures of us having fun!"

Ida let out an indignant huff, but she was grinning as she prodded Hanna in the ribs. Soon Magda joined in their play-fight, and the three of them giggled as Hanna finally pulled

Ida and Magda toward their bedchamber. Just as they raced through the door, panting, they flew smack into their governess. She looked stately in her starched brown dress with her hair wound into a roll behind her head.

The girls tumbled in all directions, but Madame Olga was a fortress. She stood sternly, arms crossed, waiting for them to get up and compose themselves.

"Young ladies," she said, sighing. She made a show of smoothing her dress, though none of the girls had ever seen a wrinkle in any item of her clothing. "Where have you been? I have been trying for years to teach you all to carry yourselves in a manner befitting your station."

The girls straightened up quickly, but they had to stifle yet more giggles as their polar bear cub, Oskar, bounded into their chamber, fresh from playing in the snow, and shook his wet fur all over them.

"Goodness me! Control that bear, girls!" cried Madame Olga, brushing snowflakes off her sleeves.

"Go and sit in the corner, please, Oskar," Magda said to the excited bear cub, trying not to laugh again.

Hanna ran a hand through her hair. "Madame Olga, have you had word from Mother and Father yet?"

The lines on the governess's face softened. She shook her head, and then gave the girls a rare smile.

"I'm certain your parents will be back any moment now, in good time for the festivities. It's not every day that their daughters turn twelve!" She turned briskly. "Now, there's no time to waste," she announced. "It's time to prepare for your birthday celebration. The people of Nordovia expect to see three elegant young ladies today, and that's what they're going to get."

Madame Olga clapped her hands together, and then waited with her fists on her hips as Ida, Magda, and Hanna formed a line. Several ladies-in-waiting rushed busily into the room.

"The dresses, Madame." One of the ladies-in-waiting held out an arm draped with bright material.

Before the girls knew what was happening their everyday dresses were whisked away, and they were helped into long, shimmering gowns. A mirror in an ornately carved wooden frame stood nearby, but the girls looked at one another instead.

"These dresses! They look like enchanted waterfalls!" Ida ran her hand over the silvery silk.

"Like sunshine on snow," breathed Magda, smoothing down her golden dress.

"Like . . . like . . . Oh, I don't know—but they're beautiful!" added Hanna, twirling around, the red silk of her gown flashing in the light as she spun. Her sisters giggled.

"Their hair," commanded Madame Olga, clicking her fingers.

One of the ladies-in-waiting slid behind Ida with a hairbrush and pulled out the tangles in her long blond hair,

and then nimbly wound it on top of her head. Hanna winced as her own hair was brushed. Her lady-in-waiting winced too, trying to arrange the short choppy red hair into something elegant. Magda squirmed as her pigtails were undone, her brown hair falling in tangles around her face as her lady-in-waiting set to work.

At last, the girls were ready. Madame Olga led them to the mirror, where they stood side by side.

Ida's silky hair had been woven with tiny pink flowers. "Mountain mist!" she exclaimed, recognizing the blossoms.

Hanna's hair was the greater miracle. Somehow it had gone from a choppy tangle to a sea of gentle waves, which had been crowned with a delicate golden tiara. Magda's hair was styled into two intricate buns at the sides of her head. Her lady-in-waiting had wound them

with threads of beautiful silver leaves.

Hanna took a step but caught her foot in her dress and had to grab Magda for support. "I can barely walk!" she complained as Magda shrugged her off. "It's a lovely dress but it's no good for having fun!"

Ida felt like she could wear her dress forever. She felt like a princess.

Soon the girls were strolling through the courtyard, their arms linked. Banners swung in the breeze, and musicians played. Everyone they passed wished them a happy birthday. The girls smiled at each well-wisher, nodding their thanks.

"Hurry up," urged Hanna, pulling Ida and Magda along. "I want to see if they've laid out the gifts yet. . . ."

Magda held up a finger. "Listen."

Two stable boys stood nearby, heads bent together, whispering.

"The celebrations are nearly set to begin,"

one of them was saying. "Seems an awfully long time to be gone at Icefloss."

"And not like Freya and Magnus at all," the other agreed. "What if—"

The rest of his words were lost beneath the circling melody of a flute.

Ida looked anxiously at her sisters.

"Never mind them," Hanna reassured her. "Mother and Father will be here any minute. Maybe they're planning to surprise us!"

The girls were distracted by a com-motion in one corner of the courtyard—a bustle of feathers

and squawking. It was the castle falconer's apprentice, Gregor, arriving to take part in the festivities. There was no mistaking him, even from a distance. His jacket was decorated with a line of bright feathers: the bold scarlet of a quetzal, the deep blue of a macaw. On his outstretched arm perched a beautiful golden-brown eagle, flapping its large wings as it stretched. Gregor murmured to it soothingly.

Magda grabbed her sisters' hands. "Come on! Let's go and see the eagle up close."

"Fine. But stop pulling!" said Hanna with a smile.

But before they had gone more than a few steps Madame Olga appeared.

"Young ladies, you must take your places. The birthday celebrations are about to begin!"

Chapter Two

All eyes were on the three sisters as they made their way through the gathering crowd, and took their seats on a platform towering over the packed courtyard. Madame Olga sat just behind them.

"The entire island is watching you, girls," she murmured. "Sit still and show that you're enjoying the festivities." Her voice softened, though it seemed to contain a hint of worry. "I'm sure your parents will be here shortly."

The land's most celebrated singer performed a traditional ballad about the Ever-changing Lights shining over the Nordovian Sea. Then swirling dancers took the stage, followed by a tumbling troupe of acrobats. Two jugglers hurled flaming sticks at each other, catching them deftly. The crowd roared with delight.

Then, cutting through the crowd's applause, came an eerie howling.

Every head in the audience swiveled toward the sound.

"Father's wolves!" the sisters shouted together. If the white wolves were back, that surely meant their parents were back too!

But the wolves that arrived in the courtyard were not standing loyally beside their master. They were alone.

And then they caught the girls' scent and raced toward them through the crowd, which spread this way and that to let the white wolves pass. They leaped up the steep wooden steps and skidded to a halt in front of the triplets. The larger of the two walked forward. His fur gleamed with ice droplets in the sunlight.

"Why isn't Father with them?" Ida wondered out loud.

The wolf looked at her, and then he bowed his head and placed something at the girls' feet.

"What's that?" asked Magda.

Ida understood first. She shivered as she realized what it meant.

"No," she said. "It can't be—"

Magda slowly reached her hand toward the wolf, patting

his head before picking up his offering from the ground. She gave a gasp of recognition.

It was their father's glove.

Hanna reached to take it from her sister, but she wasn't fast enough. Captain Vladimir, their father's deputy in the Nordovian Guard, rushed forward. He held the glove high to examine it. Oskar, the polar bear cub, loped over and stood protectively by the girls.

"The glove does indeed bear the Auroras' emblem," announced Vladimir.

A shocked murmur spread through the people who'd heard his words, and rippled out to the edges of the crowd. People got up from their seats and stood there, unsure what to do. A young child started crying.

"We must form a search party at once!" declared Captain Vladimir, his voice raised. Some of his men sprang from the crowd, awaiting further orders.

Madame Olga began to guide the girls across the platform toward the steps. "Come," she said. "The guards will do their work. They will find your mother and father very soon." She led them through the east passage and up to their chamber, and instructed a chambermaid to help them out of their gowns.

"Right then, young ladies, I think it's best if you stay safely in your room. I'll have a servant bring dinner up to you," Madame Olga told them. "The banquet will have to be canceled, of course."

The girls nodded. Their plans for the celebration already seemed so distant.

"Can't we help, somehow?" asked Hanna.

Madame Olga reached out and drew all three girls close. For the first time ever she hugged them.

"The best thing you can do is stay out of the

way," she said, but then added softly, "and try not to worry."

Then she stepped back and smoothed down her dress. "I must help put together provisions for the search party." She turned crisply and left the room.

❄

Later that night, as Oskar dozed next to the low fire in their chamber, the girls sat beside him, cuddled together under the blanket from Ida's bed. Their eyes all rested one thing. In the center of the room, on a delicate wooden table, was their most cherished possession: a snow globe that had once belonged to their mother. Many years ago Freya had given it to them. The glass felt so smooth and cold to the touch that at first they had believed it to be carved of ice. Inside, by some magic, soft snow whirled constantly around a tall crystal-clear waterfall that dropped straight into a bright, blue sea. When the girls woke each morning it was the first thing they looked at, and it brought them a feeling of happiness and peace.

"I can't stop thinking . . . ," began Magda.

". . . about Mother and Father," finished Hanna.

"I know," said Ida. "What could have happened? Just thinking of them somewhere in the forest . . ." She trailed off, and for once neither of her sisters completed the sentence for her.

The girls sat quietly for a while. Ida reached for her sketchbook and looked at the picture of the snow orchid she had begun earlier that day. It seemed so long ago now, but she found that drawing always helped to calm her nerves. She picked up a charcoal and added the finishing touches to it in the low firelight, feeling an odd tingling in her hands as she did.

"Why hasn't the guard sent word yet?" Magda wondered aloud eventually. "It's been hours."

Hanna drew the blanket closer around her

shoulders and stroked Oskar's warm fur. "I'm sure Captain Vladimir is doing his best." She wondered if Magda and Ida noticed how hollow and unconvincing her voice sounded. The fire was burning low and, even with her eyes adjusted to the dark, she couldn't make out the expressions on her sisters' faces.

Then, all of a sudden, a warm, glowing light bathed the room. Hanna could see Magda and Ida as clearly as if a bright moon had risen right beside them.

"What's happening?" Ida sat up and threw off the blanket.

"It's coming from the snow globe!"

Hanna was up and halfway to the table before her sisters could join her.

Now they stood before it, their night-dresses reflecting its milky glow. Within the glass globe, snow continued to whirl around the waterfall, but the girls could just make out another image through the snowflakes. It almost looked like . . .

A face. A face like their own.

And then a voice spoke.

"My dearest girls," the voice said, soft but clear.

The sisters drew in their breath sharply. They all leaned closer to the globe, their eyes wide.

"Mother!" they cried together.

"I do not have much time, my darlings. I am so sorry to have missed your special birthday celebrations, but something terrible has happened!"

Tears of worry slid down the girls' faces. For once none of them could speak. They just listened to their mother's familiar voice and watched the light pouring from the globe. Instinctively they moved closer together.

The voice grew stronger. "I have been Keeper of the Lights for many years, a role that you girls will one day inherit. But when I was younger my sister, Veronika, was meant to help me protect the Everchanging Lights' magic. Unfortunately Veronika didn't want the responsibility, only the power. She wanted to steal all of the Lights' magic for herself, even though she knew this would throw our beautiful island into darkness and chaos. She became the Shadow Witch, and she learned many dark spells to help her in her quest for power.

"It took all the power I had to stop her. I used a special spell to banish her to the peak of Svelgast Mountain, and I thought we were safe—but she has managed to escape. She has kidnapped your father and me, and she's placed a curse upon us that means she can drain my powers and take them for herself. I'm fighting as much as I can, and I'm using what magic I still have to reach you now. . . ."

Ida linked her arms through Magda's and Hanna's. The three sisters did not take their eyes from the snow globe.

"Listen closely, girls. Veronika wants the magic of the Everchanging Lights for herself, just as she always did, but I managed to protect it before she could trap me. I put it into three special orbs and scattered them across the island."

The sisters moved closer to the globe, their arms still linked. They could each see the others' faces, eyes wide, in the soft glow. None of them dared to speak. None of them wanted to break the spell. They all knew that what was happening was real, and yet they were afraid it was a dream.

Their mother's voice grew even more urgent.

"My daughters, you must find these the orbs. Collect them from their places of safety and bring each of them here. The Lights' magic can then be kept safe in the snow globe. And once you have found all three of the orbs you will have the power to rescue your father and me."

Hanna found her voice. "We will find them, Mother!" she cried. "We promise!"

The light from the snow globe seemed to

grow deeper just for a moment. "You must hurry, though. The orbs can only hold the magic of the Everchanging Lights until the Day of the Midnight Sun."

"The day the sun never sets," whispered Ida. "That's just a few weeks from now."

The Day of the Midnight Sun was the sisters' favorite time of year. The holiday marked the high point of the sun's long march from the depths of winter, when it barely rose above the horizon. On the longest day of the year the courtyard whirled with festivities under a sky that never grew dark. But now the day took on a new significance.

Their mother's voice went on.

"The Day of the Midnight Sun brings strong magic. The Shadow Witch knows this, and—be warned—she also knows that as Auroras you three have come into your own magic today, on your twelfth birthday, just as she and I did. She will do everything she can to stop you, to find the orbs herself, and to take over the entire island of Nordovia."

"No!" cried Magda, as Ida and Hanna shook with horror. They could not imagine their beloved land overtaken by an evil power. It could not be. It *must* not be. They were determined to stop the Shadow Witch and free their parents!

"Tell us, Mother. How can we find the orbs

if they're scattered across the island?" said Ida.

But time was running out fast. Their mother's image was getting harder to see. Snowflakes whirled around it, obscuring her features and her red hair. Soon all the girls could make out were her emerald-green eyes.

"She's fading!" Magda exclaimed. "Mother!"

Chapter Three

The sisters stared intently as the light from the globe began to die.

"The first orb you must find," the voice in the globe said urgently, "is hidden in the nest of a snow hawk. These birds are rare—but there is only one in all the land that is pure white with a silver tail."

"But where will we find the nest?" Ida asked. The girls peered into the globe, but its light was fading fast.

"Please, tell us where we can find it, Mother!" Hanna cried desperately, but it was too late. In a moment the globe looked as it always had. The light had gone.

Magda, Ida, and Hanna looked at one another, frozen with anxious wonder. Oskar paced between them nervously, and Magda reached down to pet his head.

Hanna, finally, spoke. "The silver snow hawk's nest is out there somewhere. *Somehow*, we have to find it!"

Ida walked to their large window and drew back the velvet curtain to look at the sky. The Everchanging Lights were flickering from their usual brightness to a sick, dull gray.

"But how? We've never even been much beyond the castle," she said. "What if it's dangerous out there?" She gestured toward the expanse that lay beyond their knowledge.

"It's going to be dangerous right here in the castle if Veronika the Shadow Witch has her way," replied Magda. "Everything depends on us. *Mother and Father* are depending on us."

Ida shivered. She walked back to her sisters, and they reached for one another's hands. Moonlight streamed through the opened curtains.

"The question is," said Hanna, "where do we start? How are we ever going to find that snow hawk and its nest? It could be any-where!"

Magda wrinkled her forehead, thinking. "Wait a minute. When I was watching the falconer rehearse a display with the birds last week, Gregor told me that he'd seen a snow hawk glide right over his camp in the forest. He said they like to nest at the tops of large trees. They must live in the deep forest."

"The forest is huge!" said Ida. "How would we know where to go? We could get lost!"

"We won't get lost," argued Magda. "I remember where Gregor's camp is from when Madame Olga took us there on a nature lesson. If we head toward that, then the place that the snow hawks like to nest can't be far away. And the silver snow hawk should be easier to spot than other birds."

Ida sighed, then nodded. "Okay. Let's wait till morning, and at breakfast we'll ask one of the servants to take us to Gregor's camp. Perhaps one of Captain Vladimir's men could—"

"*Breakfast?*" demanded Hanna. "A *servant?* Ida, we can't wait until morning. There's no time to lose! And we can't have anybody else from the court involved. They can't help us."

Ida frowned. "Why? They've always helped us. With everything."

Hanna put a hand on her sister's arm. "This is different, Ida. You heard what Mother said. We're going to be the Keepers of the Lights one day. This is our duty. We have to go, and we have to go alone, before anybody tries to stop us."

Ida took a deep breath. Hanna was right. She wished she could find the courage to be more like her sisters.

"Hanna has a point," said Magda. "This is

our responsibility, and there's no way the servants or Madame Olga would let us do this if they found out. We'll sneak out tonight."

"Oh! An adventure!" Hanna smiled despite herself. "Let's get dressed quickly." She flung open the doors to their giant wardrobe. It was bursting with velvet day dresses and shimmering gowns. Hanna pushed these aside and reached to the back. "Our riding outfits!" she said triumphantly. "They're warm and practical. Perfect for a quest."

"Brilliant!" said Magda. "Now we just have to make our way out to the woods."

"We'll have to be careful, though. If we wake anyone while we're sneaking out . . . ," Ida trailed off, uncertain how to finish.

"We'll just say we have a stomachache from the food this evening," said Hanna, "and we got lost trying to find a servant to help us!"

The girls smiled at one another, a flicker of

the old fun creeping into things. But then their faces grew serious.

"We'd better get changed," said Ida softly, and her sisters nodded. They laid their soft nightdresses on their beds, and pulled on their thickest, longest underwear. Then they put on their riding outfits and laced up their sturdiest boots. Soon they were ready.

Magda's hand trembled as she reached for the handle of their chamber door. As she eased the door open Oskar stuck his nose in the gap and tried to lead her out.

"Oskar!" Magda whispered to the polar bear, pushing him behind her. He looked up at her with his big brown eyes. "Oh, okay, you can come too, boy. But be very quiet!"

"Are you sure? I hope

it won't be too dangerous for him," whispered Ida.

"He's a magical polar bear, Ida! Stop worrying!" Hanna reached to pull her sister through the doorway. But just then, out of the corner of her eye, she spotted something on the floor of the bedchamber. "Wh-what's that?"

Magda and Ida turned to see, in the dim light from the fire, a large orchid lying on the floor by Ida's bed. Despite the flowers usually being a vivid pink, this one was a cloudy gray—a charcoal gray!

Ida took a tentative step toward it. "I . . . I think it's the orchid I drew," she whispered incredulously. How had it come to life? She walked over and grasped a large petal between her fingers.

Magda's eyes widened, and she grabbed

Ida's arm. "It must be your power, Ida! You can make your drawings come to life!"

Hanna laughed. "I think you're right, Magda. Quick, Ida, grab your sketchbook and pencils. We might need your power on our quest!"

Astonished, Ida picked up her drawing things and tucked them snugly inside her riding jacket. The three sisters tiptoed to the door and, with Oskar at their heels, they crept out into the passage. Hanna took one last look at their warm, cozy bedroom before she quietly pulled the door closed behind her and turned to the dark hallway.

"We'll have to try to make our way through the forest on foot," she whispered to her sisters. "Hopefully the snow won't be as deep once we reach the woods. . . ."

Ida's stomach lurched at the very idea of what her sister was saying, but she followed

Hanna and Magda down the staircase, easing open the heavy door that led to the courtyard. They peered around it carefully before dashing out through the cold night toward the gates that marked the boundary of the castle. As they ran, Oskar raced ahead of them and began to magically grow in size—Nordovian polar bears had always had this special ability. But as he was still a pup his magic was a bit unpredictable, and he didn't always know when it was best to use it. The girls knew that now was a bad time!

"Oskar, no!" hissed Ida. "Don't grow now, boy." The bear shrank again and bounded back to the girls eagerly.

Though it was dark they knew the way, and they made it over to the shadows by the gates, gulping the icy air—but they froze as they heard footsteps nearby. The girls crouched low in the darkness and saw a familiar swinging step coming close to them. It was one of their father's guardsmen on patrol! They waited until he was out of sight before they let out their breath and started to ease the gates open as quietly as they could.

Magda stopped and put out a warning hand to her sisters. She had had an idea. "Oskar is stronger and faster than us, especially if he grows bigger. What if we could get one of the transport sleighs, and he could pull it? We'd get around much quicker."

Ida nodded. "Quick, let's sneak to the wagoner's shed and get one."

The shed was a small wooden building which stood a short distance across the courtyard. The moon lit a path that had been trodden through the snow, and the girls rushed across it, with Oskar following closely.

Just then, from behind the shed, they heard the deep rumble of men's voices.

"Guards!" hissed Ida. "Get down!"

She, Magda, and Hanna dived into the snow. The cold stung their faces. There was nothing to hide behind. Ida bit her lip anxiously as Oskar lumbered away from them. What was he going to do?

The guards came to a halt nearby, and the girls heard them talking.

"I thought I heard something. . . . Oh, it's just you, boy. I'm sure you miss Freya and Magnus too, eh? We're going to find them. Don't you worry."

They heard the guards' footsteps moving away, but the sisters waited, burrowed down in the snow, until they were sure they had gone. Then they cautiously stood up and brushed the snow from their wet clothes as best they could.

"Good boy, Oskar," whispered Magda as the bear trotted back to them.

"He distracted them for us!" said Ida softly, smiling at her sisters in the moonlight.

Quickly, they made their way to the shed, Oskar at their side.

Hanna reached for the metal latch, but it was stiff and wouldn't give.

"Come on, Hanna," urged Magda.

Hanna tutted at her sister. "I'm trying!" She focused on the latch, pulling as hard as she could, but it still wouldn't budge.

"The guardsmen will be back any minute," hissed Ida.

Hanna huffed and let go of the latch, staring at it to try to see if there was another way to pull it loose. For a moment she felt a strange tingling behind her eyes, and as she stared, she was almost certain the latch shifted a little of its own accord. She grabbed it again, and was finally able to wiggle it loose and open the door!

"Phew!" she whispered. The girls slipped quickly into the dark space, and for a moment they stood there blinking. Oskar sneezed.

Ida pointed to a corner. "Sleighs!"

The three of them began to heave a sleigh from the shed, their hearts beating fast—they had to get out of there before the guard patrol came back. With Hanna and Magda pushing and Ida pulling, they managed to haul the sleigh out into the snow. A leather harness and a heavy wool blanket lay across the bottom. They latched the shed door shut again, buckled the harness around Oskar, and crowded into the sleigh.

"Let's go, boy," Magda whispered. "*Now* you can get bigger!"

Oskar looked around at the girls, then suddenly took off at a brisk pace, growing magically in size as he went, and pulling the sleigh easily. They slid through the castle gates and finally they were out into the night!

The girls pulled the blanket over their laps and huddled together beneath the coarse snow-soaked fabric of their clothes.

"We're going to do it!" Hanna whispered to Magda and Ida as they gripped one another's hands.

Magda nodded emphatically. "We're going to find the orb, and save our parents. . . ."

". . . And the island!" Ida finished.

Chapter Four

The sleigh slipped through the moonlit forest. Silvery evergreen trees, their needles slick with ice, towered over the girls. The forest grew denser as Oskar pulled them deeper into it. The girls could smell the sharp, fresh scent of pine and the warm musk of the blanket. They heard little except the crunch of Oskar's heavy paws on the snow and the rasp of the sleigh's blades. Now and then an owl's eerie hoot pierced the cold night air.

"The sky's darker now," Ida observed, shivering and pulling the blanket closer around her legs.

"I think it's because the forest is getting thicker. The trees are blocking the moonlight," Magda pointed out. She, too, shivered. "Don't hog the blanket, Ida!" she complained, but she was secretly very glad to have her sisters on either side of her.

"We should be getting to Gregor's camp soon," said Hanna, sounding more confident than she felt. "I'm almost sure I remember this stretch of forest from the time we visited his camp with Madame Olga. We went right by this part of the woods."

"Really? You must be excellent at recognizing trees," said Magda. "They all look the same to me!"

"All right, all right. But I do think we need to head east now," Hanna continued, squinting at the sky through the trees, trying to locate the North Star. "I'm sure we headed east that day."

"No," said Magda. "The sun was at our backs that morning, not ahead of us. We headed *west* through the woods."

As Oskar ran on between the dark, dense trees, Ida glanced around. Everywhere looked exactly the same to her. The cold moonlight reached the ground in a few places, making the frost sparkle. But mostly she just saw tall, silent trees full of shadows. She suddenly trembled. "We're totally lost, aren't we?" she asked her sisters.

"Of course not!" said Hanna firmly. "It's a clear night, and I see the North Star. We're heading in the right direction, I think. If we're not, we'll just change direction, that's all."

Ida groaned in frustration. She closed her eyes briefly, hoping that she might wake up

from this strange dream. But when she opened
them they were still in the sleigh. *Which is
exactly right*, she reminded herself firmly. They
were on a mission to save Mother and Father.
They couldn't do that while tucked up in bed,
and now that her magic had begun to appear
she might be able to help.

"Don't worry, Ida. We'll find the camp
soon enough," said Magda, trying to soothe
her sister. But then a high-pitched howl made
them catch their breaths and huddle together
beneath the blanket.

"It's only an Arctic fox," gasped Hanna.
She tried to make her voice strong, but it
sounded thin in the blast of cold air that
whipped their cheeks. "Probably just lost its
way, like us. . . ."

"I thought you said we weren't lost!" cried
Ida. "I knew it! You just rush into things—"

"Stop it!" shouted Magda. "Either way—"

Something heavy crashed ahead of them, and the girls were thrown forward as the sleigh halted with a dull thud.

"Oskar!" cried Magda, struggling out of the sleigh. "Hanna, Ida! Oskar's stuck!"

The sisters hurried out of the sleigh and rushed to the bear's side. A large tree had fallen across the reins between Oskar and the sleigh, pinning them down in the thick snow. Oskar was struggling to free himself, and growing in size as he panicked and thrashed around.

"Easy, boy, easy," said Magda, trying to soothe him, but the reins were straining against the polar bear and he was getting ever more distressed. "We have to do something," she said to her sisters, tears of worry in her eyes.

Ida looked around, desperately hoping to see something that they could use to free him. But instead, in the distance, she saw a shadow move between the dark trees.

Ida grasped Hanna's arm. "Look!" she whispered, the terror she felt making it hard to speak. A dark figure was slowly approaching, scarcely visible in the dim light.

Hanna gasped. "We have to free Oskar! He can protect us," she said.

A growl rolled through Oskar's throat. He struggled and fought, his front paws churning the air, but the leather harness didn't break.

Magda was desperately pulling at the trapped reins. "Ida!" she called. "Can you use your magic to draw something that might help?"

Ida frantically glanced around for ideas but shook her head. "Like what?"

The figure was coming closer through the trees. Hanna could see its breath misting the freezing air around it. She sank her hand into Oskar's thick fur, trying to think. She crouched down to where the reins were caught, right underneath the heavy tree trunk. She pushed on the trunk, hoping to move it away enough to free the panicking bear.

"Help me push!" she said to her sisters. All three pushed as hard as they could, but it was no use.

"I'm scared," whispered Ida.

Magda hugged Oskar, trying to calm him. "We'll think of something."

Hanna concentrated on the tree trunk, hoping to find some other way of freeing him.

Then, suddenly, like when she'd been trying to loosen the latch to the shed, she felt a strange tingling sensation behind her eyes. Taking a breath, she concentrated, and focused her eyes on the tree trunk. To her amazement, it started to move.

"Hanna? Wh-what's happening?" Ida stuttered.

Both she and Magda stood open-mouthed as Hanna concentrated harder.

"I . . . I'm moving it!" Hanna murmured. "I think this might be my power!"

Sure enough the tree creaked as one end lifted a tiny bit above the snow. Magda ducked down and freed Oskar's reins before Hanna blinked, and the tree slammed back into place.

"That was amazing!" said Hanna. "I can move things with my mind—heavy things!"

Ida frowned. "Well, as long as you don't blink!"

Magda quickly untangled the distraught polar bear from the reins and harness.

Realizing he was free, Oskar leaped forward and began running toward the approaching figure.

Chapter Five

As the huge polar bear neared the shadowy figure, a bird's screeching cry made the girls catch their breath. The sound seemed to come from the direction of the figure. Then *several* birds were calling, and as the figure reached the nearest trees, Magda saw that it was a boy, and the moonlight flashed on a shiny blue macaw's feather on his jacket.

"Gregor!" she cried. A flood of relief rushed over her.

But Oskar didn't understand. He stood between Gregor and the girls, the fur on his back raised.

Magda ran to the bear and placed a soothing hand on his side.

"Easy, boy," she whispered. "It's okay. It's Gregor. He's not an enemy!"

Hanna and Ida ran to their sister's side. They each placed a palm on Oskar's enormous back, their hands sinking into his thick fur as they spoke to him in reassuring tones.

"We're not in any danger," Magda told the bear. "Don't use up all your magic!"

"Don't be afraid, Oskar," Ida added.

Oskar stopped growling and dropped back onto four paws, shrinking down to his usual size. He eyed Gregor warily, still ready to protect the girls if necessary.

Gregor walked closer, and a buzzard whirled down and settled on his shoulder, flapping his huge wings. Two falcons flew into the branches above him. Their harsh calls matched the boy's angry expression, and Magda, Ida, and Hanna's relief began to drain away as he barked, "What on *earth* are you girls doing all the way out here in the middle of the night? Your polar bear nearly attacked me!"

Hanna was the first to speak.

"Uh . . . We were . . . We're sorry . . . We tried . . . ," she began, but then she trailed off, uncertain.

Gregor stood before them, seeming taller than he had back at the courtyard, his boots planted firmly in the snow. His blue eyes were stern. The large buzzard on his shoulder eyed the girls suspiciously.

Magda took over from her sister. "We traveled into the forest, because we need—"

The sight of another enormous bird swooping down from the sky stopped her. It was a golden eagle, one of Gregor's birds of prey. Magda froze, looking at its sharp beak and yellow eyes. She felt a strange tingling down her spine as she regarded it, and quickly looked away.

"We have to find the silver snow hawk," Ida finished at last. She was relieved that they'd finally managed to say it. Why were they so anxious? Gregor was only a tiny bit older than they were. Then she realized—if Gregor decided to tell his master, the falconer, about them, they would be taken straight back home and they would never be allowed to finish their quest.

Gregor's face, dimly visible in the trickle of moonlight coming through the trees, was stony.

"Why do you need to find a snow hawk?" he demanded. "And at this late hour? You could freeze to death." His glance swept warily over Oskar, the sleigh, and the riding clothes the sisters were wearing.

"Please—" Hanna began again, but Gregor cut her off.

"Whatever you three are up to, I'll be no part of it. If my master found out I'd helped you do something dangerous, I would lose my apprenticeship. You need to return to the castle immediately."

The golden eagle reared up and flapped its wings, as though in agreement with him.

"Easy now," whispered Magda, stretching a hand toward the bird. "We won't hurt you."

Ida held her breath as she watched Magda stroke the speckled feathers on the bird's wing. To her amazement, the eagle settled down and allowed Magda to continue soothing it. Ida let out her breath.

"Please," Hanna repeated, feeling stronger now, "we need your help. It has to do with our parents. You probably heard"— she swallowed, but kept going—"that they're missing."

Gregor's face softened just for a moment. Hanna set her jaw and continued. "And it's because they're missing that we're on a quest to find a rare snow hawk—a pure white one with a tail of silver feathers."

"We need to find its nest," Magda explained, her hand still on the eagle. "And now you're here, you could help us search!"

"I know it sounds strange," said Ida, "but if we don't find it, something terrible could happen to our parents, and to the island."

To their surprise Gregor nodded.

"I'm sorry about your parents," he muttered. He regarded the girls, then glanced up at the dimming lights in the sky. "And the Everchanging Lights haven't been right since they went missing. . . . That's why I was out walking tonight. We promised the guards that we'd help to keep a patrol in the forest."

"Then you'll help us?" asked Hanna hopefully.

Gregor stood in silence.

"By morning everyone will be looking for us," Ida said urgently to Gregor. "Even if you won't help us, you won't tell anyone that you saw us, will you? We have to complete our quest."

Gregor looked at the girls for a long moment. Finally he bent his head in agreement.

"I won't tell," he said. "And . . . I will help you find the silver snow hawk."

The girls looked at one another in relief.

"Thank you!" Hanna remembered to say, and the others echoed her quickly.

Gregor nodded once, then turned and began to make his way through the trees. The girls hurried to their sleigh to put Oskar back in the harness. As he heard them arguing about who would steer, Gregor looked over his shoulder and let out a gruff laugh. "Oh, you'll have no use for that where we're heading. The woods we'll be going through are too dense to navigate by sleigh. We go on foot."

He walked briskly away, letting out a short whistle that prompted the birds to fly up off their perches and follow him.

The girls looked at one another.

"On foot?" repeated Ida, wide-eyed.

Hanna was the first to jump off the sleigh. "Don't be such a baby, Ida. You heard him," she said as her boots sank into the deepening snow. She pulled one foot out with a bit of a wobble. "Do you want to find the orb or not?"

Ida frowned and jumped down from the sleigh after her sister. "Of course I do!" Then her eyes twinkled and she reached down for a stick. "But we should at least be prepared! Wait a second while I try something."

She waited for the tingle to return to her hands, and then, using the stick, she began to draw something in the thick snow. Magda jumped down from the sleigh and put her hands on her hips. "What on earth are you doing, Ida? This is no time for a drawing."

"I think you might be wrong there," Ida replied. She pointed at the ground and laughed in delight. "It worked!" There in the snow was a pair of white snowshoes, their outline barely visible against the snow. Ida slid one foot into each and grinned triumphantly at her sisters.

Hanna winked at her sister. "Well done, Ida! Now, how about you draw a pair for the two of us as well, and we can get going? We'll lose track of Gregor soon!"

Magda watched as Ida drew them each a pair of snowshoes and crossed her arms

impatiently. "Well, I'm happy that you've both got such useful powers," she muttered, "but when am I going to see if I even have *any* magic?"

Hanna shrugged and Ida gave Magda a quick hug as they stepped into their snowshoes. Then, with Oskar lumbering eagerly at their side, they quickly walked after the young falconer. They were on their way to finding the first orb!

Chapter Six

"To be honest, I think Madame Olga would have something to say about Gregor's manners," Magda whispered as they caught up with him, crossing the snow easily now in the shoes that Ida had made. The girls chuckled, imagining their governess lecturing the bird handler.

"And she certainly wouldn't like us trekking through the snow!" added Ida.

"She would demand that Gregor take us to

find the snow hawk in Nordovia's finest sleigh, with hot chocolate breaks every half an hour!" said Hanna, and the three of them laughed again, but the laughter faded. Madame Olga and hot chocolate felt very far away.

"Hurry up, you three!" called Gregor, sounding irritated. The girls hurried after him, with Oskar, back to his smallest size, bounding along beside them. They were struggling past a large snowdrift when they saw the boy standing still in a clearing ahead of them.

"What is it?" Hanna asked him.

Gregor pointed skyward, then looked up and gave a long, low whistle. The three sisters followed his gaze. They all saw it at the same time: a thin flash of silver in pure gleaming white circling far above the treetops.

"The silver snow hawk!" They gasped.

"Gregor's using a call to attract it!" Magda added, and Hanna nodded eagerly.

"I think it's working!" Ida whispered.

The bird circled lower. The girls watched it vanish and reappear as it spiraled among the pines. Gregor, following its path, ran further into the dark trees, calling it. He quickly disappeared from view.

"Come on!" said Hanna. "We're going to find that orb!"

But as she spoke, the sisters noticed something moving in the forest beside them. They strained to see more clearly.

"What's that?" Ida asked.

"Maybe it's just shadows from the trees?" Magda suggested in a tense whisper.

"No, I don't think so," said Hanna, trying to keep her voice steady. "Whatever it is, it's coming closer!"

Oskar stood near them, growling, his eyes fixed on the shadow too. The girls could see that he sensed a threat as much as they did.

They clutched hands as the dark shape emerged from the trees. The girls could make out four legs and a sweeping tail.

"A wolf!" screamed Ida.

The enormous beast stalked toward them, its head hunched low between its shoulder blades, its heavy paws crunching deep into the snow. It stood so close that the girls could feel the beast's hot blasts of breath. The three sisters huddled together, and Oskar moved in front of them protectively.

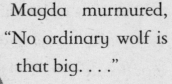

Magda murmured, "No ordinary wolf is that big. . . ."

"It has to be the Shadow Witch's magic!" hissed Hanna.

The wolf suddenly narrowed its

angry red eyes and bared its sharp teeth, its snarl getting louder. The beast seemed to grow even larger and more terrifying as its fierce gaze fixed on them.

An icy breeze began to gust through the forest. It drove shivers through the drifts of snow and rattled the needles of the pine trees, and as it grew stronger a cold, harsh voice blew into the girls' ears.

"You won't defeat me," it whispered. "Give up, and I may let you live."

The girls locked arms, frozen with fear as a swirl of icy air surrounded them.

"You know who I am," said the voice. "Your aunt Veronika, the Shadow Witch. I spied you traveling through my woods, and though the tree I felled didn't stop you, my friend here will ensure that this is the end of your adventure."

The wolf drew its snout into a sneer, hold-

ing them in the gaze of its mean blood-coloured eyes. They knew they couldn't outrun it. They could hear the rumbling growl in its throat, and

Ida gasped in horror as saliva slid from its mouth into the snow.

Oskar started to grow in size, but after a moment he stopped and shrank again. He turned his large worried eyes to the girls.

"Poor Oskar," whispered Magda. "You're still really young, and you've already done so much for us! Your magic must need time to replenish." The bear whimpered but bravely stood his ground between the wolf and the sisters.

The freezing wind whipped up the snow and hissed, "The Everchanging Lights and Nordovia will soon be under my power. No one can stop me! Your mother and father grow weak, and you girls are powerless!"

As the wind rose to a harsh cry, a rumble worked its way through Oskar's throat, and he lunged at the wolf. But he was no match for the beast, and with a gigantic paw it knocked him flying. Oskar yelped and slumped into a snow-drift, dazed.

The wolf turned its huge head back to face the sisters and Magda screamed, but from behind them, footsteps came crunching through the snow. It was Gregor, running back toward them. He skidded to a halt as he saw the huge wolf and his face went pale. The wolf growled and tensed its body.

"Watch out!" shrieked Ida.

The wolf sprang toward the girls.

In a flash Hanna grabbed her sisters and yanked them out of the way. They huddled together behind a tree.

At the same time Gregor leaped forward and grabbed the wolf's tail. With a huge effort he began to pull the wolf back by its fur—but with one mighty swing of its body the wolf flung Gregor into a tree.

Gregor collapsed against the trunk, trying

to catch the breath that had been knocked out of him. The girls hunched lower behind their tree as the wolf stalked toward them again.

"We have to do something!" cried Magda.

Hanna narrowed her eyes and concentrated hard on the wolf, feeling the tingling sensation from before. She gritted her teeth, and managed to push the wolf, sending it

stumbling back. But in a second the wolf righted itself and turned back to the sisters, ready to pounce.

"Run!" cried Magda, and the girls scattered.

The wolf darted between Magda and

Ida, teeth flashing, hot breath churning. It snapped at Ida, who whisked the back of her riding jacket out of the way just in time. Whirling around, its fiery eyes turned to Magda and it leaped at her instead. Magda threw herself behind a tree as it sprang, and the wolf skidded to a stop in the snow before recovering itself and running at Hanna. In a flash Magda reached out and grabbed Hanna's arm, pulling her away from its jaws.

Ida, breathing hard, pointed. "Quick, we need to get up that tree! The wolf won't be able to reach us up there!"

The three sisters, their hearts pounding, the muscles in their legs shaking, pulled themselves up into lowest branches of the tree. Their hands were numb with cold and sticky with pinesap.

Hanna climbed higher, quickly and easily. "Come on!" she called down. "It can still reach you!"

They could hear the wolf snarling beneath them— but above them something white streaked through the sky and drew closer. It was the silver snow hawk! Just as the girls were looking at the bird, they heard a snapping sound from below. Teeth bared, the wolf had made a giant leap toward Magda, whose leg was still dangling dangerously from the branch.

"Watch out!" called Ida, but the wolf's sharp teeth caught her sister's boot and began to drag her down. The snow hawk swooped low again. Magda felt the strange tingling down her spine, just as she had when she'd encountered Gregor's golden eagle earlier. She locked eyes with the snow hawk as it flew toward her, and the tingling got stronger. Suddenly she felt herself floating up into the sky.

Down below, she heard her sisters cry out in surprise.

Hanna's voice carried toward her. "Magda?"

Magda felt a
strange buoyancy as
she moved her arms . . .
not her arms . . . wings!
Somehow she was soaring into the sky beside
the snow hawk. She looked left and right, and
realized she was flapping magnificent white
wings. The trees below got smaller, and she
laughed in surprise, but instead of her laughter
she heard the wild cry of a bird.

"Magda!" Hanna shouted again. "You . . .

you've turned into a bird! You've turned into another snow hawk!"

Ida gave a laugh, half shocked, half excited, and shouted up to the sky too, "You've got your power!"

Chapter Seven

Magda flew through the sky after the silver snow hawk, who seemed to be circling back toward the top of the tree where her sisters were still clinging, while the wolf snarled and paced below. The bird was coming to land on a cluster of branches near the top of the tree. Magda landed on a branch nearby just in time to see the hawk settle onto a nest. That was it! That must be where their mother's orb was hidden!

She fluttered closer, and, sure enough, she could

see the glowing pink
orb inside the hawk's
nest. She let out
another squawk,
trying to alert
her sisters, but she
knew they wouldn't
understand. How could
she get the orb out of the nest when all she had
were claws? How long would she stay a bird?
But, as if in answer, she began to feel another tingling sensation down her spine. She flapped her
wings a little, experimentally, but found them
becoming less light and more like . . . arms! She'd
turned back into a girl—and as she clung to the
branch she realized just how high up she was!
Perhaps being able to turn into an animal wasn't
as much fun as she thought. But it did mean that
she was able to get to the orb.

Carefully, holding tightly to the branch,

Magda whispered soothingly to the snow hawk, hoping it wouldn't attack her as she gently eased the pink orb out of the nest. She'd done it!

"Ida! Hanna! I've got it!" she called down to her sisters, who were balanced in the branches below her.

"Amazing!" she heard Hanna call back. "Can you climb down to us?"

Magda wasn't sure—she wasn't as good at climbing as Hanna. But she took a deep breath, tucked the beautiful, gleaming orb inside her riding jacket, and began to tentatively climb through the branches toward her sisters.

"Careful!" called Ida, and Magda couldn't help tutting in spite of her nerves.

"Of course I'm being careful!" she shouted.

After a few nail-biting moments, she managed to reach her sisters. Cautiously she pulled the orb out of her jacket to show them. The sisters stared at the beautiful iridescent pink light flickering and flowing inside it, just like the Everchanging Lights did in the sky. They smiled at one another.

"No!" A fierce, ice-laden wind hurled itself around the tree. "That's *mine!*" it screamed.

"What are we going to do?" cried Hanna, trying to shelter from the freezing wind as she watched the huge wolf circling the base of the tree, its eyes fixed on the girls. Gregor and Oskar were still lying dazed where they'd fallen.

Ida, Magda, and Hanna peered anxiously at the scene below them. Then Ida realized something. "Wait a minute," she whispered. "That wolf is definitely in the power of the Shadow Witch. Maybe if we can break her hold over him, we would have a chance to escape!"

Her sisters nodded.

"Good idea! But how?" asked Magda.

"We use our powers, silly," said Hanna, sounding more confident than she felt. She looked around for inspiration. Suddenly her eyes lit up, and she whispered a plan to her sisters.

"Okay?" she asked. She looked at Magda, who nodded once, and then turned to Ida, who looked a little more unsure, but she nodded too.

"One . . . two . . . three . . . Go!" cried Hanna.

Ida pulled out her sketchbook and pencil from where she'd tucked them inside her riding jacket and hastily drew two slingshots. She felt the tingling in her hands as the images came to life, and she passed one of the slingshots to Hanna so that they could load them with hard pine cones from the tree. Then they began to fire them rapidly down at the wolf. The wolf snarled and shook its head, trying to shelter beneath the branches.

While it was distracted, Magda tucked the pink orb safely in a crook of the tree and took a deep breath as she tried to attract a red squirrel that Hanna had spotted sheltering nearby out of its hiding place.

"Here, little one," she said, struggling to see the little creature through the pine needles, not even sure if this would work—but once she caught its eye she felt the tingling down her spine again.

"I . . . I think it's working! But I don't know how long it will last," she cried to her sisters just as she felt her body becoming lighter and lighter. She glanced down and saw paws. Little red paws! She leaped down from the tree, dancing between the branches and—gathering all her courage—sprang onto the wolf's back and bit down hard on its ear! She was so tiny and agile that before the wolf could turn on her she'd jumped away, and as it chased her she raced toward a huge old tree, its many branches heavy with snow.

Hanna concentrated on the branches of the tree. As the wolf ran beneath them she used her magic to shake them hard and sent a huge heavy sheet of freezing snow down onto the beast. Magda leaped to the safety of the next tree just in time.

The avalanche fell on the wolf with a loud *flumph*! As the beast disappeared beneath the snow, the cold wind howled like an angry scream then suddenly died, and the woods became silent. The wolf was buried for a moment, but then its nose slowly reappeared, snuffling through the snow. It clambered out of the snowfall, blinking in confusion and shrinking before the girls' eyes. Now a normal wolf, it took a dazed look around then ran off. And not a moment too soon, as Magda found herself turning back into a girl. She jumped down from the tree, panting hard.

"We did it!" cried Hanna, placing the orb safely in her jacket as she and Ida climbed down and ran over to Magda. "Well done, us!"

"Is the Shadow Witch gone? Are we safe?" asked Ida.

"When we knocked out her power over the wolf, she lost this fight," said Hanna. "I think we're safe for now."

"Look at Oskar!" cried Magda.

The little polar bear cub was slowly scrambling to his feet. He shook himself all over. Once he was sure of himself, he leaned, growling, in the direction the wolf had gone.

"It's okay, boy," Hanna told him with a grin.

"We took care of ourselves," explained Magda, stroking his fur.

"With the help of a little magic," finished Ida.

The three of them turned to Gregor, who was also stumbling toward them, clutching his shoulder. "I can't believe it," he murmured, "I think I've been seeing things!"

Magda chuckled, looking at her sisters. "We could never have found the snow hawk's nest without you!" she said to him.

Hanna cleared her throat dramatically. "On behalf of our parents, and all of Nordovia, we thank you," she concluded formally. The other girls nodded, smiling, and they took his hands.

Gregor looked down at the snowy forest floor, embarrassed. "It was nothing," he grunted.

Hanna clutched the precious pink orb inside her jacket. "We need to get back to the castle," she said. "Can you take us to our sleigh, Gregor? Even if Oskar stays quite little and goes slowly, if we leave now and help to push the sleigh, we might be able to get home before dawn!"

Gregor led the way back, and the girls harnessed Oskar to the sleigh. They all helped push-start it, and once the bear had picked up speed they jumped inside and waved good-bye to Gregor. They could hardly believe the adventure they'd been on.

At last, just as an early dawn light began to creep into the sky, they emerged from the woods and Oskar raced down to the castle gates.

"Quick, now, while the guard patrol is on the other side," said Ida softly. They jumped down from the sleigh, quietly slid back through the gates, and returned the sleigh to the wagoner's shed. They crept back into their bedchamber just as sunlight began to break through their window.

Hanna carefully pulled the pink orb from her jacket, and together the girls walked over to the snow globe, which was beginning to glow again.

"Mother?" said Magda softly. "We did it! We found the first orb!"

The globe shimmered more brightly, and

they heard their mother's voice faintly from within it. "Well done, my darling daughters! Now place the orb next to the snow globe, and watch. . . ."

Hanna, Magda, and Ida each clasped their hands around the pink orb and moved it toward the snow globe, holding their breath. They gasped as the glittering orb was magically absorbed into the swirling snow of the globe.

"The magic of the pink light will be held here for safekeeping," their mother told them. The light in the globe began to dim again. "But don't forget," warned Freya, her voice getting more and more faint, "you must find the other two orbs before the Day of the Midnight Sun!"

"Mother?" said Ida anxiously. But it was too late. She was gone. For now . . .

The girls looked at one another, eyes wide.

"Well, at least we've found one of the orbs," said Magda, and her sisters nodded.

"And we'll find the others as soon as we can!" Hanna finished.

Oskar settled down by the fireplace, huffing gently into a well-earned sleep. The girls changed out of their cold, stiff riding outfits and gratefully put on their soft, warm nightgowns. But despite getting into their beds they remained wide awake.

"That was the most exciting thing we've ever done!" whispered Hanna.

"It was a bit scary sometimes," Ida whispered back.

"I know. But we did it—together," Magda replied.

"Soon we'll have all the magical orbs," said Hanna, her voice starting to sound sleepy.

"Then we can stop that nasty Shadow Witch

once and for all. . . . ," said Magda, sounding tired too.

"And free Mother and Father!" Ida finished with a yawn.

The girls smiled, each bathed in the faint glow of the early morning. They knew it wasn't going to be easy finding the other two orbs—not with the Shadow Witch determined to stop them. But they had discovered their magic, and they were ready for their next adventure, whatever it might be!

The adventure continues in
THE CRYSTAL ROSE

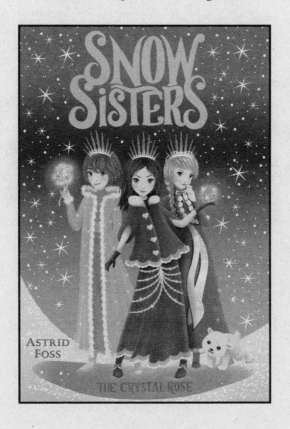

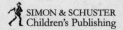 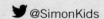

READ & LEARN

with *simon* kids

Keep your child reading, learning, and having fun with Simon Kids!

A one-stop shop where you can
find downloadable resources, watch interactive author videos, browse books by reading level, and more!

Visit us at
SimonandSchusterPublishing.com/ReadandLearn/

And follow us @SimonKids

SIMON & SCHUSTER
Children's Publishing
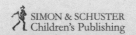

Mermaid Tales

Join Shelly and her mermaid friends in all of their exciting adventures under the sea!

#1 TROUBLE AT TRIDENT ACADEMY

#2 BATTLE OF THE BEST FRIENDS

#3 A WHALE OF A TALE

#4 DANGER IN THE DEEP BLUE SEA

#5 THE LOST PRINCESS

#6 THE SECRET SEAHORSE

#7 DREAM OF THE BLUE TURTLE

#8 TREASURE IN TRIDENT CITY

#9 A ROYAL TEA

MermaidTalesBooks.com

Candy Fairies

Chocolate Dreams

Rainbow Swirl

Caramel Moon

Cool Mint

Magic Hearts

Gooey Goblins

The Sugar Ball

A Valentine's Surprise

Bubble Gum Rescue

Double Dip

Jelly Bean Jumble

The Chocolate Rose

A Royal Wedding

Marshmallow Mystery

Frozen Treats

The Sugar Cup

Sweet Secrets

Taffy Trouble

The Coconut Clue

Rock Candy Treasure

A Minty Mess

The Peppermint Princess

Mini Sweets

Visit candyfairies.com for games, recipes, and more!

EBOOK EDITIONS ALSO AVAILABLE

FROM ALADDIN · SIMONANDSCHUSTER.COM/KIDS